Hello Kitty®

The New Friend

By Elizabeth Bennett
Illustrated by Sachiho Hino

SCHOLASTIC INC.

New York   Toronto   London   Auckland   Sydney
Mexico City   New Delhi   Hong Kong   Buenos Aires

ISBN 0-439-87136-0

12 11 10 9 8 7 6 5 4   9 10 11/0

Printed in the U.S.A.
First printing, September 2006

 and got off the 🚌.

😺 was waiting for them.

"How was 🏫?" she asked them.

"Today was okay," answered 🐱.

"But tomorrow will be better."

"Why?" asked .

" said there will be a new

girl in our class,"  told .

"And my class is getting a !"

said .

When it was time for [bed],

[cat] read [Hello Kitty] and [Hello Kitty]

a [book].

[cat] looked at the [clock]

and turned out the light.

"Sweet dreams," [cat] said

as [Hello Kitty] closed her [eyes].

After a yummy breakfast

of and ,

 grabbed her

and ran to catch the .

 got on the , too.

 found a seat next to

her friend 🐑.

They talked about the new

girl at 🏫.

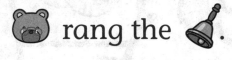 put away her 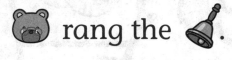 and

put her 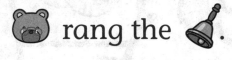 on her .

 rang the .

"Class, this is Connie,"

said .

", there is an empty

next to ."

 looked at with a big

smile on her face.

At lunchtime,  looked

for 🐑.

They ate lunch together every day.

🐱 couldn't believe her 👁 👁.

🐑 was sitting with 🐼 and

there was no room for 🐱 at

the lunch 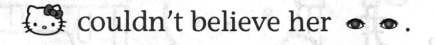.

She ate her lunch and drank

her 🥛 by herself.

went to the playground.

Sometimes she and 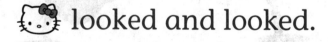 played

at recess.

Sometimes they went on

the 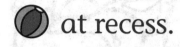.

Where was ?

looked and looked.

Finally she saw her.  was

sitting by the big 🌳 .

She was talking to 🐼 .

Tippy and Kathy were there, too.

🐱 did not go over to them.

Her friends were busy with 🐼 .

They weren't looking for 🐱 .

 felt sad.

She thought it would be fun

to have a new girl in  , but

she wasn't having fun.

She missed  .

 looked at the  on the wall.

She couldn't wait for the

to ring.

At home,  told  about .

"All my friends played with .

No one played with me."

 gave the girls  and .

"Why didn't you ask to join them?"

 asked.

 couldn't think of a good reason.

The next morning,  put on

her 🎒 and climbed onto the 🚌.

" !" called 🐑. "We saved you

a seat."

🐱 looked down the row. She saw a

seat for her right between 🐑 and

🐻. Now 🐱 was happy to see

her best friend . . . and her new

friend!

Did you spot all the picture clues in this Hello Kitty book?

Each picture clue is on a flash card. Ask a grown-up to cut out the flash cards. Then try reading the words on the back of the cards. The pictures will be your clue.

Reading is fun with *Hello Kitty*!

Mimmy

Hello Kitty

Mama

school

hamster

Mr. Bearly

Papa

bed

clock

book

pancakes

eyes

backpack

milk

Fifi

bus

bell

desk

table	Connie
swing	ball
cookies	tree